All Those Secrets of the World

by
JANE YOLEN

Illustrated by
LESLIE BAKER

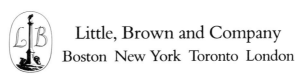
Little, Brown and Company
Boston New York Toronto London

To my cousin Michael Garrick
and my brother Steve Yolen,
who may not remember,
but they were there.

J.Y.

In memory of my father,
Kenneth Leslie Baker

L.B.

First Paperback Edition

Library of Congress Cataloging-in-Publication Data

Yolen, Jane.
   All those secrets of the world / by Jane Yolen;
illustrated by Leslie Baker.
      p.   cm.
   Summary: When four-year-old Janie's father goes off to war, the rest
of the family moves to the grandparents' home on the Chesapeake Bay,
where Janie learns a secret of the world which helps her understand her
father's long absence.
   ISBN 0-316-96891-9 (hc)
   ISBN 0-316-96895-1 (pb)
   [1. Fathers and daughters — Fiction.]   I. Baker, Leslie A., ill.
II. Title.
PZ7.Y78A1   1991
[E] — dc20   89-14003

10 9 8 7 6 5 4 3

Paintings done in watercolor on Strathmore Bristol.

Color separations made by Colotone, North Branford, Connecticut.

Text set in Bembo by Litho Composition Company, Inc., Boston, Massachusetts,
and display type set in Diana by Typographic House, Boston, Massachusetts.

Printed and bound by Worzalla, Stevens Point, Wisconsin.

Published simultaneously in Canada
by Little, Brown & Company (Canada) Limited

Printed in the United States of America

$\mathcal{M}$y cousin Michael was five
and I was four
when my father went off to war.
We were allowed
to go down to the docks
to see the big ship sail off.
Daddy gave me a hundred
butterfly kisses
and whirled me around and around.
Then he hugged everyone once
and Mama twice before going on board.

Hundreds of grown-ups crowded around,
waving handkerchiefs and crying.

I got to hold a little flag.
I waved it so hard,
the stick broke in two.
Mama tucked the flag
into my pocket
and warned me not to fuss.

From somewhere on the ship
Daddy threw more kisses,
at least that's what Grandma said.
But even from my perch
on Grandpa's shoulders,
I couldn't find him.
There was a band playing
"Over there, over there,"
with a tuba making oompah-pahs.
Mama sang along.

Slowly the ship moved away
and the dock seemed to shake.
Dirty waves slapped the posts.
Grandpa bought us ice cream cones,
chocolate with jimmies,
and Grandma used her handkerchief
to wipe our mouths and hands.
Michael got lost in the crowd.
We had to get a policeman to find him.

But everyone had a good time,
except Mama,
who cried all the way home,
and my baby brother, Stevie,
who slept through it all.

The next morning Mama didn't get up
to make me breakfast,
and Grandma said, "Hush, let her sleep."

So Michael and I
went down to the long beach
that ran from Kecoughtan Road
all the way to Newport News,
where the waves lapped
black and greasy
onto the graying sand.
We'd been warned not to swim
in the Chesapeake
because it was so dirty with oil.
But Michael said to take off
our shoes and socks.
Wading wasn't swimming, he said.
They'd never know, he said.
The water was cold,
and we walked hand in hand.

"Look!"
I pointed at little specks
moving on the horizon.
"Are those birds?"
"Those are ships," Michael said,
"taking soldiers across the sea to war."
I shook my head.
Those *couldn't* be ships.
"My daddy went on a *big* ship.
Those specks are no bigger than my thumb."

Michael smiled down at me
and dropped my hand.
"I'll tell you a secret of the world,
the kind you'll know when you're older.
They only look small
because they're so far away.
Stay right here and watch."
He ran down the beach,
leaving a trail of wet footprints.
When he was far away, he called,
"Am I small now, Janie?"
I nodded because he was
no bigger than my hand.
He ran farther down the long beach.
"Am I smaller now, Janie?"
He was the size of my little nail.
"Come back, come back," I cried,
suddenly afraid he'd disappear forever
like the ships gone from the horizon,
dropped over the edge of the world
where no policeman could ever find him.

After we threaded our way home
through the whispering sycamores,
the grown-ups knew we'd been in the bay.
We had black greasy rings
around our ankles
and my sunsuit was spotted and damp.
Michael got a spanking
because he was older.
All I got was a long soaking
in Grandma's lion-paw tub.
I sat there till the water was cold
and I was covered with bumps.
We both got a story at bedtime.
Once upon a time, it began;
happily ever after, it ended.

My cousin Michael was seven
and I was six
and my baby brother, Stevie,
just starting to talk
when my father came home from the war.
There were no big ships
or waving flags,
just a stranger in brown
with his arm in a sling
unfolding himself from a cab.

Everyone cried, except Mama.
When Daddy tried to kiss her,
Stevie yelled,
"Go away, you bad man,
don't you touch my mama."

So Daddy stopped kissing her
and picked me up instead,
in his good arm.
"You're so big, Janie," he said.
"Lots bigger than I remembered."
His eyes were the blue
of the sky above us
and there were sharp creases
at their edges.
Throwing my arms around him,
I spoke Michael's secret in his ear.
"That's because you were
so far away, Daddy.
When you are far away,
everything is smaller.
But now you are here,
so I am big."
"Of course," he said.
"I knew that."

He gave me a hundred butterfly kisses.
We whirled around and around
under the whispering sycamores
until neither one of us
could tell big from little,
young from old,
short from long,
peace from war,
all those secrets of the world.